GORMY RUCKLES
MONSTER HERO

Guy BASS
Illustrations by Ross Collins

■SCHOLASTIC

Look out for other monster adventures:

GORMY RUCKLES
Monster Boy

GORMY RUCKLES

GORMY RUCKLES
Monster Birthday

GORMY RUCKLES
Monster Contest

Meet the Ruckles

(And hope that they've already eaten)

Gormy Ruckles, the monster boy, was very small, very blue and very hairy. He had a long tail and just one quite good fang. Gormy lived at No. 1 Peatree Hill with his mother, Mogra the Horrid, and his father, Grumbor the Grim. It was the only house on Peatree Hill. In fact, it was the only house for miles...

...well, would *you* want monsters as neighbours?

To Uncle Selwyn,
the real best uncle in the world

First published in the UK in 2009 by Scholastic Children's Books
An imprint of Scholastic Ltd
Euston House, 24 Eversholt Street
London, NW1 1DB, UK
Registered office: Westfield Road, Southam, Warwickshire, CV47 0RA
SCHOLASTIC and associated logos are trademarks and or registered
trademarks of Scholastic Inc.

Text copyright © Guy Bass, 2009
Illustrations copyright © Ross Collins, 2009

The right of Guy Bass and Ross Collins to be identified as the author
and illustrator of this work has been asserted by them.

Cover illustration © Ross Collins, 2009

ISBN 978 1 407 10852 0

A CIP catalogue record for this book is available
from the British Library

Printed in the UK by CPI Bookmarque, Croydon
Papers used by Scholastic Children's Books are made from
wood grown in sustainable forests.

1 3 5 7 9 10 8 6 4 2

This is a work of fiction. Names, characters, places, incidents
and dialogues are products of the author's imagination or are used
fictitiously. Any resemblance to actual people, living or dead,
events or locales is entirely coincidental.

www.scholastic.co.uk/zone

OnE

The Big Rain

It was a bright, cloudless afternoon in late
Maytober, and Gormy Ruckles was busy
thinking about tomorrow's monstering
lesson. His father, Grumbor, had decided
to test his knowledge of every one of his
How to be a Better Monster lessons
so far, from Lesson One-and-a-bit –

Remember You're a Monster – to Lesson Six-Hundred and Ninety-Nineteen – Never Forget You're a Monster.

Gormy wondered how he could possibly remember everything he needed for the test. He stared nervously out of the window, and spotted his father standing on the front lawn. Grumbor was one of the most monstrous-looking monsters ever. He was bigger than ten cows tied together and covered in thick, blue fur. As Gormy wandered outside to join him, he noticed that Grumbor was staring into the sky and shaking his head.

"What are you looking at?" asked Gormy.

"I felt a twinge in my toeclaws," said Grumbor. *The Big Rain* is coming."

"The Big Rain? Really?" squealed Gormy, looking up. He couldn't see anything but clear, blue sky.

"My toeclaws are never wrong. Look there," said Grumbor, pointing to a single, grey cloud, growing larger and darker by the second. It swirled and churned as if it was alive. "And we all know what that means. . ." he added, grumpily.

"Uncle Kruckles is coming to stay!" Gormy shouted with glee, and ran back into the house. It was the most excited he'd been since he'd thrown his first rock! The Big Rain came at about the same time every year. More rain fell in one night than in all of the other nights put together. But it wasn't the rain that Gormy was excited about. It was the fact that every time the Big Rain came to the valley, so did his Uncle Kruckles!

"Mum, Uncle Kruckles is coming!" exclaimed Gormy again, as he dashed into the kitchen. His mother, Mogra, was busy preparing lunch. Mogra was almost as big as Gormy's father, but much more pink and a good deal jollier.

"I know, your father's been twiddling his toeclaws all day! Why do you think I'm cooking all this extra food?" she said, popping four just-stomped goats into the oven. "You know how much Kruckles likes his goats."

Gormy felt like he was going to explode with excitement (which was rare but not unheard of amongst monsters).

As far as he was concerned, Kruckles Ruckles was the best uncle (and the best monster!) in the world. He was even more monstrous than Grumbor, with two ridiculously impressive horns and so much bright red fur that he could have donated half of it to the Society for the Bewigging of Balding Beasts and still been the hairiest monster ever.

What's more, Uncle Kruckles monstered wherever he wanted, whenever he wanted, and didn't let anyone tell him what to do. He didn't even have a house – he just slept in caves or under the stars, so that he never missed a chance to monster. Except when the Big Rain came – it was the one time of year Kruckles would seek shelter on Peatree Hill.

"He should be here any time now – he usually arrives before the Big Rain starts—" began Gormy's mother, but she was interrupted by a loud thunderclap. A second later, the skies opened and the rain began to fall.

"It's started! But . . . but he's not here! What if he's not coming?" cried Gormy, suddenly panicking.

"I'm sure he'll be here soon," said Mogra. "Now, why don't you go upstairs and check all the windows are shut, while we wait?"

Gormy raced upstairs, by now terribly concerned that Kruckles wasn't going to show up. Had he found somewhere better to stay? The thought was too horrible to contemplate. Gormy set about closing the windows, each time looking out to see if he could see Kruckles coming. He had just reached his bedroom window when he heard a small, gruff voice.

"Room for a small one? I'm close to drowning out here!"

"Mike!" said Gormy, as his best friend crawled in through the window. Mike was a scuttybug, and like all scuttybugs, he hated the rain, mainly because it tended to wash away any traces of his favourite food, poo.

"Is your uncle Kruckles here yet?" Mike asked as he scuttied on to Gormy's nose.

"No, and he always comes before the Big Rain! What if he's off on some amazingly monstrous adventure and he's forgotten all about us?" Gormy replied.

"Don't worry, Gormy – you know how Kruckles likes to make an entrance. He'll probably be here any second now," chirped Mike.

And a second later,

BOOOM!!!

Two

Kruckles Ruckles

Something crashed through the ceiling! A massive shape fell to the floor next to Gormy, bringing most of the roof down with it!

"**Aaaah!**" screamed Gormy, leaping out of the way of the tumbling rubble. He scampered to the far corner of his room and crawled under a chest of drawers.

"What in the name of the Great Dung Heap was *that*?" squeaked Mike. "Is the sky falling in?"

"I don't know," whispered Gormy nervously, as the Big Rain poured in. In the centre of the room, he could see a huge, imposing shape. Gormy held his breath as it began to move.

"By the talking trees of Willow Wood, what a landing! I hope I didn't squash anyone important. . . " said a voice that sounded like hot lava flowing down a mountain. It was unmistakeable.

"Uncle Kruckles!" shouted Gormy.

"Gormy? That can't be you, can it?" said Kruckles as he got to his feet and dusted the debris out of his fur. "Look how much you've grown since I last saw you! Why, we're almost the same size!"

Gormy puffed up with pride at the
thought of having grown at all, but in fact,
he was still no bigger than Kruckles' little
fingerclaw. His uncle was even bigger than
Gormy remembered – much taller than his
father and at least twice as fat!

"What did you . . . how did you. . ."

gasped Gormy, staring up at the enormous hole in the ceiling.

"What? Oh, yes, sorry I'm late. I was battling a family of dragons on Goggan Moor. Once we'd settled our differences I convinced one of them to give me a lift, so **WHOOSH!** off I went through the air! As soon as I spotted Peatree Hill below me, I hopped off and here I am!"

"You rode on a *dragon*?" cried Gormy, staring through the hole in the ceiling to see a long, snake-like dragon soaring across the rain-filled sky.

"Of course – it's the only way to travel! That reminds me, did I ever tell you about the time I battled the Seven Serpents of Sorrow Marsh?" Uncle Kruckles began, as Gormy's mother and father crashed into his room.

"Gormy! Are you all right? What happened?" cried Grumbor.

"Grumbor, you old rock-lobber! How about a hug for your not-so-little brother?" bellowed Kruckles, grabbing Grumbor and squeezing him tightly.

"Kruckles . . . so you did make it, after all," grumbled Grumbor. "Still making a mess wherever you go, I see. . ."

"Mogra, my dear! How do you put up with this grump? If you ever get sick of his belly-aching, you just let me know!" said Kruckles, with a wide, five-fanged grin. "And can it be? You look even *more* hideous than when I last saw you!"

"Oh, Kruckles, you sweet-talker," giggled Mogra, blushing a deep pink.

"Uncle Kruckles, this is my best friend, Mike," said Gormy, holding Mike up as high as he could. Kruckles leaned forward and squinted his eyes.

"What am I looking at, exactly?" he asked.

"Hello there," said Mike.

"A scuttybug!" exclaimed Uncle Kruckles. "Well, I'll be a monster's uncle! I bet you taste awful."

"I do, sir, I really do," said Mike, rather proudly.

"Excuse me," interrupted Grumbor, his ears steaming with rage. "But am I the only monster whose noticed that you've *wrecked Gormy's room*? There's rubble and water everywhere!"

"Oh, don't get your tusks in a twist, Grumbor – wrecking things is what monsters do. You don't mind, do you Gormy?"

"Nope!" said Gormy, happily, as a huge piece of ceiling rubble floated by his feet. As long as Kruckles was here, he didn't mind if the sky really did fall in!

"Well, all this monstrousness has given me an appetite! I could eat a dozen goats and still have room for snake pie!" bellowed Kruckles, slinging his sack over his shoulder.

"It's funny you should say that. . ." said Mogra, winking at Gormy.

Three

Monsters Don't Need Lessons

Twenty-two minutes later, Uncle Kruckles had devoured (often without chewing):

- THIRTEEN ROASTED GOATS
- ONE PEELED COW
- SEVEN OTTERS - ON - A - STICK
- TWO GALLONS OF STOAT SOUP

🐾 FOUR PLATEFULS OF TOAD-IN-THE-HOLE

(made with real toads)

🐾 EIGHT SLICES OF SNAKE PIE

(with lashings of newt sauce)

🐾 HALF A HALF-BAKED HOOMUM

Gormy had never seen any monster eat
so much! Finally, Kruckles sat back in
his chair and let out the almightiest burp
Gormy had ever heard,

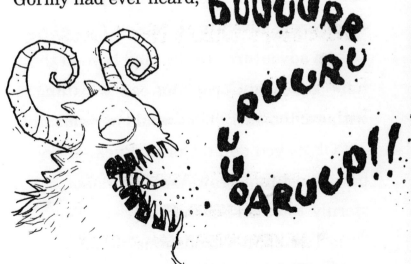

BUUUURRUUURUUOARUUP!!

"By the Cliffs of Lunacy, that was the most monstrous meal I've had all year – and last week I ate through a mountain!" said Kruckles, patting his huge red belly.

"So, how long are you planning on staying *this* time?" asked a disgruntled Grumbor.

"Long enough to spend some quality time with my favourite nephew, of course!" said Kruckles. "So, Gormy, how about tomorrow I take you on a proper monstering adventure?"

"An adventure? In the land beyond the hill?" squealed Gormy, his ears whistling with excitement. "That would be *amazing*!"

"Oh no you don't, Gormy Ruckles. You have a test tomorrow," said Grumbor, sternly. "Lesson Seven Hundred – The True Test of Monstrousness."

"But. . ." began Gormy.

"Lessons? You're not still bothering with that nonsense, are you?" laughed Kruckles. "Monsters don't need lessons! We're monsters, monstering is what we do naturally!"

"It's not that simple—" began Grumbor, angrily, but Kruckles interrupted.

"You know, Gormy, when your father was a monster boy, he used to spend all day with his snout buried in his **How to be a Better Monster** book. But not me! I didn't waste a second learning how to be a monster – I just got out there and did it! And I turned out pretty monstrous, wouldn't you say?" Then he let out the most almighty **ROOOAARG!**

"You didn't have any monstering lessons? But you're the most monstrous monster *ever*!" said Gormy, easily as impressed as he was deafened.

"Ha! You're just saying that because it's true! So how about it, Grumbor? Don't you think it's high time that Gormy got to see the *fun* side of monstering? No books, no lessons, just some old-fashioned scaring and smashing?"

"I said no," said Grumbor, getting up from the table with a teeth-rattling thump. "What if you ran into a situation you couldn't handle?"

"Impossible! I can handle anything, and so can Gormy . . . which reminds me,

I forgot to give you your present!" said
Kruckles, reaching for the large sack
by his side. Gormy's eyes bulged
with excitement – Uncle
Kruckles' presents were
always astonishing,
unpredictable things
from some far corner of
a distant land.

His favourite presents so far were:

A TWISTED TRICK-STICK FROM THE
KING OF THE HOP-GOBBINS

A LOCK OF HAIR FROM THE ONCE-WAS-
WICKED WITCH OF WORMLING COVE

A TOOTH FROM POGUM OGUM, THE
LIVING SWAMP

Kruckles reached into the sack and

rummaged around. "Aha – got it! Now close your eyes and hold out your paws!"

Gormy closed his eyes tightly and held his paws out. After a second, Kruckles shouted, "Open!" Gormy opened his eyes . . . and was confronted by an enormous bear!

"**Aaah!**" he screamed, as Kruckles dropped the bear on top of him!

He'd never seen a real, live bear before, never mind been squashed by one! It was three times bigger than he was, and at least four and a half times as heavy!

"Isn't he adorable? I thought he'd make a nice pet!" said Kruckles, cheerfully. "He's been in that sack for ages, so he'll be angry *and* hungry – a perfectly monstrous combination!"

The bear scrambled to its feet and began running around the kitchen, crashing into a chair and knocking it over! Gormy leaped out of the way as the chair crashed to the ground in front of him.

"Well, he's certainly lively," said Mike, scuttying on to Gormy's shoulder.

"What were you thinking? You can't give Gormy a bear!" growled Grumbor as he tried to catch it.

"Why not? A bear is the *perfect* present for a really monstrous monster boy, right Gormy?"

"I . . . I . . . yeah!" said Gormy. He had to admit, it was by far the best present he'd ever been given, even if it wouldn't stop crashing around the room. He decided that the polite thing to do would be to introduce himself to the bear (and hopefully calm it down a bit) so he leaped in front of its path and said, "Hello, my name's Gormy Ruckles. . ."

Unfortunately, this simply drove the bear to attack. It chased a screaming Gormy around the kitchen and out into the hall.

"See? He wants to play 'chase'!" added Kruckles.

Four

Pursued by a Bear

After exiting the kitchen pursued by a bear, Gormy raced through the hall, into the sitting room, back out of the sitting room, and into the study. The bear ran angrily after him, grunting and growling.

"He's gaining on us!" cried Mike from Gormy's shoulder. It struck Gormy that, despite all his lessons, he still seemed to spend more time running away from things than running after them! Maybe his uncle was right about lessons, after all. . .

"Go away! I'm not allowed any pets! Especially ones that try to eat me!" yelled Gormy as he darted into the study and ran around the enormous desk. The bear wasn't listening. It charged towards Gormy at full speed.

"Eaten by a bear . . . I can honestly say this is not how I thought it would end," said Mike with a shrug. Gormy looked up at the enormous bookshelf next to him. It was his only chance – he leaped on to it and started climbing up the books! He clawed his way up an enormous copy of *Monstrous New World* and on to the next shelf. Then he climbed up *Pride and Monstrousness, Monstering Heights* and *Harry Monster and the Goblet of Goats*. He was halfway up a copy of *Coping With Unmonstrousness* when he looked back. The bear had started to climb as well! It dragged itself up the books by its claws, and was moving at an incredible speed!

"He's right behind us!" cried Mike, now a little nervous. Sure enough, the bear was only one book away! Without thinking, Gormy pulled the nearest book off the shelf.

"Hey, bear! How about a little light reading?" shouted Gormy, and threw the book!

KLOMP!

It landed on the bear's nose! The bear lost its balance and fell to the floor with a **THUMPH!** A second later, Grumbor and Mogra burst into the room, closely followed by a chuckling Uncle Kruckles.

"There you are! Are you all right?" said Grumbor, grabbing the dazed bear in his massive claws.

"I'm . . . I'm great!" cried Gormy, beaming from pointy ear to ear.

He'd never had
such a monstrous
present in his entire life. It
was better than a million of Pogum Ogum's
teeth (which was nearly a whole mouthful!).
In fact, it was probably the best present
ever! "Can I keep it? Can I?" he pleaded.

"What? No, of course not! You're not
ready for . . . for bears!" growled Grumbor.

"Of course he is! Gormy can handle
anything," said Uncle Kruckles, picking
up the book that Gormy had thrown at the

bear. He chuckled and held it up. "And would you look at this! It looks like Gormy finally found a good use for monstering books!"

Gormy looked at the book. On the front it said: How to be a Better Monster by Grumbor Ruckles (aged one fifth and one sixth).

"And what's more," continued Kruckles, "I think he's proved that he's monstrous enough for a real adventure! What do you say?"

Gormy held his breath with anticipation, and crossed his claws.

"It couldn't hurt, you know," said Gormy's mother. "Gormy has been working very hard lately – he could probably afford to miss one lesson and have a little fun. . ."

"Please, Dad! I won't get into trouble, I promise!" begged Gormy. Grumbor sighed and rubbed his eyes.

"Fine," he said. "You can go with your uncle for one day and one night, and no more. After that it's straight back to the hill, and straight back to lessons."

"Thanks, Dad!" cried Gormy, beside

himself with excitement. "And can I keep my bear?"

"No! No bears! This is a house, not a zoo!" cried Grumbor. He looked around for somewhere to put the bear, but he couldn't see anywhere. He shrugged, popped it in his mouth and swallowed it whole.

Five

The Adventure Begins

After a night full of monstrously
adventurous dreams, Gormy woke up
feeling even more excited than he did
on Muffaluffmas Day (which is like
Christmas Day but all the presents are
alive). He hopped out of bed and jumped
into the pool of water that was once his

room (his father had patched the hole in his ceiling with two trees from the garden, but it was still letting in monster-sized drips) and packed his backpack for the adventure ahead. Then, after a breakfast of cow-tail crumpets, Gormy and his uncle, and of course Mike, set out on their adventure.

"Have a good time, my little furball," called his mother, as she and Grumbor waved them off. "And do *try* not to get into trouble."

"I won't!" said Gormy, rather hoping that he would.

"And if you run into problems, remember your lessons!" Grumbor shouted after them.

"Oh, stop fussing – Gormy's in safe claws with me! We'll be back by next sunrise!" boomed Kruckles.

As they set off down the hill, the ground was still wet from where the Big Rain had fallen. Gormy followed Uncle Kruckles through the ring of trees that surrounded Peatree Hill and emerged in the land beyond the hill. The valley had been turned into a river! Gormy could no longer see the bottom of the hill – in fact, he couldn't see the valley at all. It was completely submerged, with only the tops of the tallest trees poking out from beneath the water.

"How will we get off the hill?" said Gormy, suddenly worried that they would have to have their adventure in the garden!

"We're not going to let a little water stop us!" laughed Uncle Kruckles. He picked up Gormy and lifted him all the way up to the top of his head. "Hang on tight, we're going for a swim!"

Gormy barely had time to grab hold of Kruckle's head-fur before he began stampeding down the hill! Faster and faster he ran, until they were almost at the water's edge, and then he leaped into the air! Gormy held his breath and **SPOSHOOoooOOOooOSH!!** They plunged into the water!

Gormy gripped Kruckles' fur for dear life as he was completely engulfed – he even saw a fish swim past his face! After what seemed like a fifth of forever (but was probably only a second or two), they bobbed back up to the surface. As Kruckles rolled on to his back, Gormy crawled down his face and on to his fat belly.

"Wha – what happened?" said Mike, crawling out of Gormy's backpack and spitting out a mouthful of water. "I thought I made it clear that scuttybugs and water don't mix!"

"That was great!" giggled Gormy, shaking the water off his fur like a wet dog. "Can we do it again?"

"All in good time, my boy. There's a whole world out there, and it's ours for the monstering!" said Kruckles, as they floated down the river of rain-water.

Gormy stared out at the flooded valley, then up at the faraway cliffs and mountains. The land beyond the hill seemed bigger and more exciting than ever before.

"Where are we going, Uncle Kruckles?" he asked.

"To wherever the river takes us," laughed Kruckles. "To adventure!"

Six

Cow - ball

Gormy, Mike and Uncle Kruckles had been floating down the river for most of the morning. They had travelled far further than Gormy had ever been. Gormy lay on Kruckles' belly, staring up at the clouds, as his uncle regaled him with tales of monstrous exploits.

They always began the same way, but each one was more spectacularly monstrous than the last. Gormy's favourites, in reverse order of monstrousness, were:

"That reminds me, did I ever tell you about the time I trampled ten towns in two days?"

"That reminds me, did I ever tell you about the time I out-yakked the Yakkum-to-Yak?"

"That reminds me, did I ever tell you about the time I accidentally ate the Ghost Dog of Grimsmoor?"

"That reminds me, did I ever tell you

about the time I thumb-wrestled the fifty-fingered Frump?"

Kruckles was halfway through telling Gormy about the time he battled the Wiggly-Woo for a wasp sandwich when, **TRRRRrrrrrrURF!**

Kruckles had run aground! The river of rain had finally started to dry up, and Kruckles had come to a halt at the bottom of a small hill. Ahead of them the land was lush and green, and above them loomed a huge mountain.

"Well, well! It appears we have arrived!" boomed Kruckles.

"Arrived where?" asked Gormy, hopping off his uncle's belly as Kruckles stood up and stretched to his full height.

"Ha! As long as there's monstering to be had, who cares where we are?"

"But what about Lesson Three Hundred and Threety-Four – Care About Your Whereabouts? Dad says a monster should always know where he. . ." began Gormy, but Kruckles wasn't listening – he'd seen something over the horizon.

"By the Crooked Claws of Krung! I spy some cows!" cried Kruckles, bounding towards a herd of brown-and-white cows, who had gathered under a large tree. "Time for a little cow-ball!"

"What's cow-ball?" asked Gormy, but Kruckles was already too far away to hear him.

"Whatever it is, I don't think it's going to be pretty," said Mike, scuttying out of Gormy's backpack and under a nearby leaf. "If you don't mind, I might sit this one out."

Gormy watched in amazement as Kruckles wrenched the large tree out of the ground. He spun it around his head and then, with an almighty swing, swatted a passing cow, launching it into the air!

"MOOOOooooooo!" cried the cow as it went flying! Gormy almost fainted at the sheer monstrousness of it all!

"What are the rules?" he asked, as Kruckles chased after the terrified cows.

"Rules? There are no rules! We're monsters!" roared Kruckles. He grabbed a large bull by the horns and threw it at Gormy, crying, "Here, have a go!"

"Uh-oh. . ." squeaked Gormy as the bull flew towards him! He looked around for something to bat it with, but the only thing he could see was a tiny twig. He lifted it up in front of his face as he saw the bull's shadow fall over him . . . **BLOMF!**

"Gmmmf-mmf!" mumbled Gormy, squashed between the ground and the bull's enormous rump.

After a few moments, Kruckles lifted the dazed bull off Gormy and tossed it into a nearby field. He peeled Gormy out of the ground and cried, "Great catch! You're a natural at cow-ball!"

"Really?" asked Gormy, spitting out a mouthful of cow-hair. He looked back at the Gormy-shaped hole in the ground. "That was great! Can we do it again?"

Gormy and Kruckles played cow-ball until they were both exhausted. Gormy even tried his hand at batting (with a medium-sized branch) and after being kicked in the head three or four times, he got quite good at it. It was the most fun he'd had all year. There were no rules, no lessons, and nothing to learn. There was just adventure! He was finally starting to feel like a real monster.

Seven

Up Close and Hoomum

By mid-afternoon, all the cow-related monstrousness had given Kruckles an appetite, and he and Gormy settled down for a spot of lunch.

"Is this what you do every day?" said Gormy, as he watched Kruckles roast a cow's leg over an open fire.

"Of course," laughed Kruckles, taking a massive bite. "I am a monster, after all."

"You make monstering look easy, that's for sure," said Mike, tucking into a cow pat dung-ball.

"It is easy, my foul-tasting little friend! When you're a monster, you just do whatever you like, whenever you like, and no one can do anything to stop you! Nothing's mightier than a monster – we're at the top of the food-chain!"

Gormy stared out over the land, and wondered why his father had never told him this. It turned out monstering was easy! He was just starting to question whether all his lessons had been a waste of time when he spotted something in the distance. Smoke, rising up from the ground at the base of the large mountain. He looked more closely, and realized that the smoke was coming from the chimney of a small house. In fact, there were *lots* of houses.

"Uncle Kruckles!" whispered Gormy with barely-controlled excitement. "Hoomums!"

"By the Bones of the Black Witch, I do believe you're right!" cried Kruckles. "What are we waiting for? Let's go and scare them witless."

"Really? N-now? In the daytime? But what about Lesson Two Hundred and Fivety-Eight – Be Frightful After Nightfall? Dad said I shouldn't approach hoomums in the day because—" began Gormy.

"Honestly, you'd think your dad didn't *want* you to be a monster! I think it's high-time the hoomums found out just how monstrous Gormy Ruckles really is. . ."

Gormy followed his uncle as he strode fearlessly towards the hoomum village. The minute they saw Kruckles coming, the hoomums started screaming and running around in fear.

"Look at them go! Silly creatures. I never get tired of watching hoomums panic!" cried Kruckles, as he tramped into the village. Gormy ran behind him as his uncle upturned horse-carts, kicked down walls and tore the roofs off houses!

"It's a messy business, this monstering," commented Mike as they watched Kruckles leap into the air and belly-flop on to a hut.

"I know . . . isn't it *brilliant*?" squealed Gormy. *Uncle Kruckles must be the most monstrous monster ever!* he thought as Kruckles stomped off in pursuit of a terrified horse, leaving Gormy alone in the village.

"Uh, Gormy?" said Mike, tapping Gormy on the shoulder with a greasy leg. "You might want to have a look at this. . ."

Gormy turned around slowly. There, standing in front of him, were three hoomums. They didn't look like "silly creatures" at all, close-up. They were at least twice as tall as Gormy and very angry looking. They paced slowly towards him, talking to each other in hushed tones. Gormy couldn't tell what they were saying (hoomum talk is too ridiculous for monsters to understand) but they clearly meant to catch him.

"Um, isn't this usually the part where we run for our lives?" whispered Mike as the hoomums got closer, but Gormy kept his ground. He was tired of running away . . . from hoomums, from bears . . . and he wasn't going to run away any more! As the hoomums were about to pounce, he took a deep breath.

GRrRRooAAG9GGH!

It was the most monstrous roar he'd ever done! The hoomums ran away screaming and flapping their arms! Gormy could hardly believe it! He'd scared away not one but *three* hoomums, and he'd never even had a lesson in how to do it!

"How's it going, Gormy?" asked Kruckles, as he rambled back into the village, juggling a couple of horrified hoomums.

"That was great! Can we do it again?" said Gormy, proudly.

"That's the spirit! It's like I always say, when you're a monster, there's nothing you can't handle! But I think we've done about all the monstering we can do here. So, where do you want to go next?" said Kruckles.

Gormy stared up at the vast mountain and grinned. "To adventure!"

Eight

The cave of the Gloam

Gormy and Kruckles had been climbing up the mountain for almost an hour. By the time they reached the top (still laughing about how much they'd scared the hoomums), the sun had begun to set, bathing the whole land in a deep orange glow. They stared out across a vast mountain range, full of high, snow-capped peaks and dark, bottomless ravines.

"Uncle Kruckles, look!" shouted Gormy, as they made their way along the top of the mountain. There, staked into the ground, was a small sign which said,

"Who's the Gloam?" asked Gormy.

"Haven't a clue!" bellowed Kruckles. "But I don't see why we should beware him. I've never bewared anything!"

A few steps further on, they came across another slightly bigger sign.

"Sounds like a challenge to me!" laughed Kruckles.

Further on, they spied a third and fourth sign, and then more, and more, and *more* . . . and each one was more alarming than the last:

VENTURE NO FURTHER! THE GLOAM LIVES HERE!

WHAT ARE YOU, CRAZY? YOU'RE HEADING

STRAIGHT FOR THE GLOAM!

CAN'T YOU READ? TURN BACK!
YOU DON'T WANT TO MESS WITH
THE GLOAM!

LOOK, YOU MIGHT BE A REALLY BIG
MONSTER BUT YOU SHOULD STILL DEFINITELY
NOT GO ANY FURTHER! I MEAN IT! THE
GLOAM IS BAD NEWS!

In fact, by the time the sun had set,
Gormy and Kruckles had counted *three
hundred and nine* signs. They happily
ignored them all and continued to the edge
of a steep ravine, with a long drop into
darkness. On the other side of the ravine
was what looked like the entrance to a
cave, and strung across the gap, was a thin,

rickety-looking rope-bridge.

"What do you think?" said Kruckles as they stood at the edge of the rope-bridge.

"What have we got to be afraid of? We're monsters!" said Gormy boldly, and stepped on to the rickety bridge.

K-REEEAK!

Gormy stopped in his tracks as the bridge creaked like an old door. He looked down between the flimsy wooden planks. The ravine was so deep that it didn't seem to have a bottom! He suddenly felt rather nervous, and gulped unmonstrously.

"It looks as sturdy as a rock! Let's go!" boomed Kruckles, and strode on to the bridge.

KREAK! KREAK! K-K-KRREEEAK!

Kruckles' massive weight shook the bridge as if it was in a tornado! Gormy held on to the bridge's ropes for dear life as it swayed and swung! Finally, Kruckles reached the other side, and the bridge began to settle. Gormy held his breath and scampered across to where Kruckles was waiting at the mouth of a huge, black cave.

"Right! Let's see what all the fuss is about, shall we?" asked Kruckles, and tramped fearlessly into the cave. Gormy was about to follow, but for some reason, he just stood outside, frozen to the spot. It was as if the world was standing still. Then suddenly, thick, black smoke began pouring out from within the cave!

"Well, that doesn't look too good," said Mike. Gormy tried to peer into the darkness, but it was darker than a storm cloud. Then came a deep rumbling, like a cross between growling and rolling thunder.

"That doesn't *sound* too good either," said Mike.

"Uncle . . . Uncle Kruckles? Are you there?" whispered Gormy, as the rumbling growl became louder and louder. Then, finally, he heard a voice from inside the cave. It was his uncle's.

"Gormy! RUN!"

Nine

The Gloam

Kruckles came running out of the cave, faster than Gormy had ever seen him move!

"Time to go!" shouted Kruckles. "I think that's enough adventure for one day!"

"What is it? What's wrong?" asked

Gormy. A second later, he got his answer.
From inside the cave, the Gloam appeared.
It was the most monstrous thing Gormy
had ever seen.

It was ten times larger than Kruckles,
and had more fangs than all of the

monsters Gormy had ever met put together. Its two huge, thick arms looked like tree trunks, and its long, thick tail was covered in a hundred and fourteen spikes, each one bigger than Gormy. If that wasn't monstrous enough, the Gloam was constantly surrounded by a cloud of darkness – with two white eyes which burned through the gloom.

"B-b-big . . . m-monster. . ." was all a terrified Gormy managed to whimper. Kruckles ran towards him, reaching out to pick him up, but the Gloam's massive claw swept down and knocked Kruckles to the ground! Kruckles bounced along the ground like a big hairy ball. He'd barely scrambled to his feet when the Gloam loomed over him.

"Uncle Kruckles!" cried Gormy.

"Run, Gormy!" he cried, as the Gloam glared at him with its fireball eyes. In fact, the Gloam's stare was so monstrous that it made Kruckles' hair turn white! Then the beast opened its huge, shadowy jaws and,

GRAAAAAARGH!

The Gloam's roar was deafening! It sounded like all the monsters of the world roaring at once as part of a sponsored roar, and it was easily the most monstrous thing Gormy had ever heard! In fact, it was *so* monstrous that it made Kruckles' hair fall out! He was completely bald!

"I have to do something!" cried Gormy as the Gloam lifted its vast foot and held it above Kruckles' head. It was going to squash him! Without thinking, Gormy picked up a nearby rock and threw it!

TONK!

It bounced off the Gloam's hide as if it was a tiny pebble, but it was enough to get the beast's attention. It fixed its burning glare on Gormy.

"I'll tell you what," said Mike, trying to stay calm, "I reckon now would be a great time to do that whole running away thing."

As the Gloam turned to face Gormy, it swatted Kruckles into a nearby tree, and Gormy's uncle fell limply to the ground. The beast roared, spewing a cloud of inky darkness into the air, and then charged towards Gormy! Gormy turned and raced towards the bridge on all fours. He could hear the Gloam's thunderous footsteps behind him, each one shaking the ground like an earthquake! Then, just as Gormy thought he might just make it to the bridge, the Gloam's massive foot crashed to the ground in front of him!

BOOOOM!

"**YAAH!**" screamed Gormy, darting to his left! The Gloam lifted his other foot and stomped again, and again and again –

BOOM!
BOOM!
BOOM!

– as Gormy weaved and dodged for his life! Gormy knew that

sooner or later one of the Gloam's stomps would squash him flat, if something worse didn't happen first! Then, as if on cue. . .

"Watch out for its tail!" cried Mike as the Gloam swung its massive, hundred-spiked tail along the ground! Gormy ducked as it whooshed over his head, but it was so enormous it created a gale, blowing Gormy up into the air!

"**YAAAH!**" he screamed again, flying through the air and landing in a nearby tree! He grabbed on to a branch and secretly hoped that the Gloam hadn't seen where he had landed.

GRAAOOOOOOR!

roared the Gloam, making every leaf in the tree dry up and fall off. Gormy looked up to see the massive monster staring right at him.

"Uh-oh," he squeaked. The Gloam roared again and tore the tree out from its roots! It lifted the tree above its head and shook it until Gormy couldn't hold on any longer. . .

"**YAAAAAH!**" he screamed for the third time that day! He was flung out of the tree, through the air, and **KRUMP!** on to a rock! By now Gormy was dazed and aching, and would happily have lain there, rubbing his wounds, but the Gloam was already stomping towards him!

"Crushed by a giant monster . . . I think I'd rather have been eaten by the bear," said Mike. Gormy couldn't believe it – his first real monstering adventure and he was about to get eaten! It made him wish he'd stayed on Peatree Hill. He remembered sitting in the study with his **How to be a Better Monster** book, leafing through the pages and trying to remember every lesson . . . and then he realized that he did! Every single one, from One-and-a-bit to Six Hundred and Ninety-Nineteen – Gormy remembered them all! As the Gloam stomped towards him, an idea popped into his head.

"Lesson Two Hundred and Two – Surprise Beats Size," he said to himself. He flexed his claws and gritted his teeth . . . and then did something very surprising.

He ran straight towards the Gloam!

Ten

Gormy Ruckles, Monster Hero

"Gormy! What are you *doing*?" screamed Mike, as Gormy ran towards the Gloam!

"I'll tell you later . . . if we make it out alive!" said Gormy. He took a deep breath into all four of his lungs and roared his most monstrous roar!

ROOAAAAAARGH!

The Gloam suddenly stopped in its tracks, and looked a bit confused! This was the first time anything had ever run *towards* it – usually everyone ran away – and this was certainly the first time anything had roared at it! The befuddled beast staggered back, not knowing what to think about this brave little monster. Perhaps it was so monstrous that it didn't *need* to be big! Gormy kept roaring and running towards the Gloam until it had staggered all the way back into its cave!

"I did not see that coming," said Mike with a surprised grin.

"He won't be gone for long – Lesson Three Hundred and Seventy-Eleven – Monsters are Never Gone for Long," said Gormy, skidding to a halt next to his uncle. "Uncle Kruckles, wake up! We have to go!" he shouted, prodding Kruckles with his paw.

"**AAAAAH! BEWARE THE GLOAM!**" screamed Kruckles, waking up. Then he looked down at his fat, bald belly and screamed again. "My fur! My precious fur! I'm naked!"

"We'll deal with that later!" said Gormy, helping Kruckles to his feet. They rushed to the rickety rope-bridge, and then made their way across

72

KREAK KREAK KREEEAK! as fast as they could. They were nearly halfway across when the sky darkened around them. . .

"He's back!" cried Mike. Gormy looked back to see the Gloam reappear from its cave and charge towards them! Gormy tried roaring again, but this time the Gloam kept coming. Within seconds it had reached the bridge!

KREAK KREEAKK KREEEAK! CRACK! KREEEEEAK! KRACK!

Gormy held on tightly as the bridge rocked and swayed with the Gloam's every clawstep! The fragile planks shattered beneath it, and one of the two ropes holding up the bridge snapped under the beast's weight!

"By the Bottomless Pit of Bottomless Bottoms!" yelled Kruckles as the bridge swayed from side to side. "There's only one rope left! If the Gloam breaks that, the bridge will split in two – we'll fall!"

"So, if the Gloam doesn't kill us, the fall will? Yikes!" gasped Mike. Gormy glanced at the last remaining rope, then at the Gloam, who was only seconds away.

"Lesson Ninety-Nine and a half – Never Fail to Use Your Tail!" he said, wrapping his tail tightly around the remaining rope. He nodded to Kruckles to do the same.

"By the Eighty Armpits of Ong!" cried Kruckles, realizing what he was planning. He wound his tail nervously around the rope and held his breath.

"Gormy, I hope you're not thinking what I think you're thinking!" said Mike.

"Hang on, Mike, we're going for a ride," he whispered, as the Gloam reached out a huge, black claw to grab them. Gormy stared straight into the beast's fiery eyes and clenched his little blue paws.

"Hey Gloam! Here's a lesson for you! Lesson Five Hundred and Fivety-Five – Expect the Unexpected!" he cried. Then he bared his one quite good fang, and bit through the rope!

"**YAAAAAHH!**" screamed Gormy. The bridge split in two, sending Gormy and

Kruckles crashing into the cliff-face with a **THRUMP!** The Gloam tried to leap for the side of the ravine, but it was too late – it fell, roaring an impossibly loud roar which faded into silence as it disappeared into the abyss.

Before long, Gormy and Kruckles had clambered up what remained of the broken rope-bridge, and out of the ravine.

"You did it!" squealed Mike, poking his head back out of Gormy's backpack.

"I *did* do it, didn't I?" said Gormy to himself, surprised at his own monstrousness.

"By the Hairy Eyes of Horg. . . I'm sorry I got us into such a mess, Gormy. I suppose there really *are* some things that are too monstrous for me to handle," said a regretful Kruckles,

but then he noticed that Gormy had an
enormous grin on
his face.

"That was great!"
said Gormy. "Can we
do it again?"

Eleven

Lesson Seven Hundred– The True Test of Monstrousness

The trip back to Peatree Hill took the whole night and another whole day. By the time they got back, Gormy's mother and father were beside themselves with worry.

"Gormy, where have you been?" cried

Mogra, squeezing him so tightly he thought he might pop.

"And why has your uncle Kruckles got no hair?" asked Grumbor.

Before long, all the important questions had been answered. After being given a thorough telling off for being so irresponsible, Kruckles settled down for a nap, carefully wrapped in a thick blanket to cover his hairless belly. Then, as Gormy's mother prepared hot goat juice for everyone, his father sat him down next to the fire.

"That was a very monstrous thing you did, saving your uncle from the Gloam," said Grumbor. "I always feared that one day Kruckles would get into a situation that he couldn't handle, but I didn't think it'd be *you* getting him out of it! Perhaps you are a little more monstrous than I give you credit for."

"I'm just glad I remembered all my monstering lessons when I met the Gloam," said Gormy.

"Glad to hear it. Then it sounds like

you're ready to take the True Test of Monstrousness!" said Gormy's father.

"The *test*? But – but I thought, I mean, after everything—" began Gormy, suddenly nervous.

"He's only joking – you don't need to take the test! You've more than proved how well you know your lessons," said his mother, handing him a cup of goat juice. "You've made us both very proud, Gormy."

"What's more, we think you've proved that you're ready for some *real* monstering," said his father, resting a large claw on Gormy's shoulder.

"Really? Out there, in the land beyond the hill?" Gormy asked, excitedly.

"Absolutely! I might come along too, though – just to make sure you don't get into *too* much trouble," chuckled his father. "So, where do you think you'd like to go first?"

Gormy took a sip of goat juice, and grinned an exceptionally monstrous grin. "To adventure!"

Look out for more **MONSTER** mayhem

GORMY RUCKLES
MONSTER BOY

GUY BASS
Illustrations by Ross Collins

MONSTER laughs!

Gormy Ruckles
Monster Mischief
monster laughs!
Guy Bass
Illustrations by Ross Collins

GORMY RUCKLES
Monster Trouble

MONSTER laughs!

Guy BASS
Illustrations by Ross Collins

MONSTER laughs!

Charlie

If you like Gormy, why not look out for my adventures!

Meet Charlie - he's trouble!

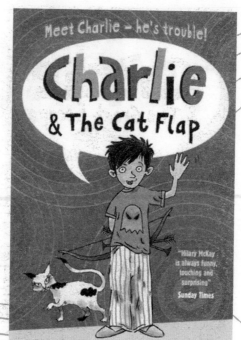

Charlie and Henry are staying the night at Charlie's house. They've made a deal, but the night doesn't go quite as Charlie plans. . .

Meet Charlie - he's trouble!

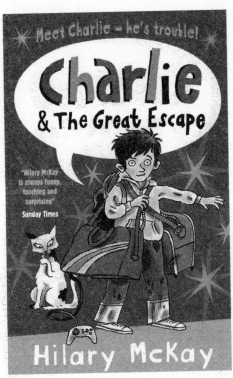

Charlie's fed up with his mean family always picking on him – so he's decided to run away. That'll show them! Now they'll be sorry!

But running away means being boringly, IMPOSSIBLY quiet…

Meet Charlie – he's trouble!

"The snow's all getting wasted! What'll we do? It will never last till after school!"

Charlie's been waiting for snow his whole life, but now it's come, everyone's trying to spoil it! Luckily, Charlie has a very clever plan to keep it safe...